KNOCK KNOCK
PIRATE

Caryl Hart & Nick East

KNOCK KNOCK!
Who goes there?

KNOCK KNOCK
PIRATE

KNOCK
KNOCK

Caryl Hart & Nick East

For Dad C.H.
For Lynn, Nick, Alex & James x N.E.

HODDER CHILDREN'S BOOKS

First published in Great Britain in 2018 by Hodder and Stoughton

Text © Caryl Hart 2018
Illustrations © Nick East 2018

The moral rights of the author and illustrator have been asserted.

A CIP catalogue record of this book
is available from the British Library.

HB ISBN: 978 1 444 92850 1
PB ISBN: 978 1 444 92852 5

10 9 8 7 6 5 4 3 2 1

Printed and bound in China.

MIX
Paper from
responsible sources
FSC® C104740
FSC
www.fsc.org

Hodder Children's Books
An imprint of
Hachette Children's Group
Part of Hodder and Stoughton
Carmelite House
50 Victoria Embankment
London EC4Y 0DZ

An Hachette UK Company
www.hachette.co.uk

www.hachettechildrens.co.uk

Hodder
Children's
Books

ONE pirate with huge purple hair!
She tilts her hat. She rubs her scar.

I say "Hi," and she says,

"Can I help you Ma'am?" I say.
"My dad is out at work today."
But the Pirate Captain strides right in!
"Where's yer treasure, Sonny Jim?"

I start to say, "My name's not Jim!"
when TWO more pirates tumble in!
The Captain grins, "Yo! Dan and Stan.
Grab all the treasure that you can!"

THREE granny pirates wearing shawls
crash through the roof on cannonballs.

BOOM!

FOUR pirate grandads with knobbly knees
comb their beards and scratch their fleas.

"Here, take this treasure map," I say.
"You can keep it if you go away.
Keep sailing till you find this dot."
The Captain smiles. "X marks the spot!

Hoist the mainsail.
Scrub those decks!

Secure the rigging.
Lift these nets!

Haul in the anchor.
Grab that bag!

Let's fly the Jolly Roger,
our pirate flag!"

The whole house shakes beneath my feet.
Then sails away along the street!
"Wait!" I cry. "Don't make ME come!
What will I tell my dad and mum?"

BOOM

SPLOSH

"Don't worry," sing FIVE pirate girls.
"Just help us find gold, jewels and pearls.
You'll be fine. Don't make a fuss.
Now come below the deck with us!"

We find SIX jolly pirate mums,
baking cakes and doing sums
while SEVEN babies in their cots
tie nappies into sailors' knots.

On and on the house-ship sails
past factories, flats and giant whales,
and out onto the ocean wide,
where monsters lurk and mermaids hide.

Suddenly the pirates yelp,
"A giant squid has grabbed us. Help!
ALL hands on deck! Attack! Attack!"
The squid squirts ink; and they fire back.

The ship is pitching to-and-fro
when a dreadful gale begins to blow.
A swirling whirlwind rages by
and sucks the squid into the sky!

"Hooray! We're saved!" the pirates clap.
"Now come on Jim-lad. Here's your map.
Please guide us to our treasure now."
"I can't," I say. "I don't know how!"

EIGHT pirates who could use a bath
press round me with an evil laugh.
"If you can't help us, Jim," they say.
"You'll walk the plank – yes, right away!"

I swallow hard. "My name's NOT Jim!
That plank's too wobbly. I can't quite swim."
NINE grizzly pirates, who don't look kind,
growl, "It's OK. The sharks won't mind."

BOING!

I edge out slowly. "Here I go!"
The sharks swarm hungrily below.
But TEN pirate children cast a net
and catch me, so I don't get wet!

Then suddenly we see below
a shimmering shining sort of glow.
"Look!" I cry. "The treasure chest!"
The pirates cheer. "Jim! You're the BEST!"

We haul the chest up from the sea.
The pirate crew ALL grin at me.
"We knew you'd do it, Pirate Jim!"
They dance a jig, and I join in!

Across the seven seas we roam
until it's time to head for home.
Then on the stroke of four o'clock
we steer our ship back into dock.

"Haul down the mainsail. Clear the decks!
Dust the rigging. Fold these nets!
Drop the anchor. Stash that bag!
Bring down the Jolly Roger, our pirate flag!"

"I'm home!" calls Dad. "Are you OK?"
"I'm all right now YOU'RE here," I say.
"Some pirates came and kidnapped me.
They sailed our house across the sea.

We journeyed round the North Pole twice!"
"Oh, right," Dad chuckled. "That sounds nice.
And now I suppose they've sailed away?"

"YES! You've JUST missed them, Dad!" I say.

PIRATE
CHILD

PIRATE
GRANDAD

PIRATE
GIRL

PONGY
PIRATE

PIRATE
BABY